Library of Congress Cataloging in Publication Data. Drescher, Henrik. Simon's book. Summary: Simon flees from a friendly monster with the aid of his drawing pens. [1. Drawing—Fiction. 2. Monsters—Fiction] I. Title.
PZ7.D78383Si 1983 [E] 82-24931 ISBN 0-688-02085-2 ISBN 0-688-02086-0 (lib. bdg.)

Late one evening,
a young boy began to
draw a story about Simon
and the scary monster.
        He became drowsy,
and instead of finishing the
drawing, the boy headed for
the comfort of his downy bed,
leaving Simon stranded on the
page with a big furry beast.
As soon as the boy was asleep,
a curious sound came from
the direction of the
drawing table.

First it was a faint shuffle,
then a louder rustle.

One by one, like caterpillars, the pens
crept out of their jar onto the drawing pad.

The bottle of ink followed.

The pens introduced themselves.
They promised to get Simon
out of the monstrous predicament
he had been drawn into so thoughtlessly.

Hello
Simon

Simon shook their tails

and introduced himself
to the ink bottle,

with a very messy result.

No sooner had Simon cleaned himself
than the beast leapt at the foursome.

The fastest pen drew a hole in the page.
They thought it would be too small for
the monster to follow through. . . .

BUT IT WASN'T!

On the next page, the creature chased
them up a rocky hill.

Simon and his friends knew a quick way
to get down.

Simon tumbled as the pens spun out of control.

The ink bottle hit the ground with a great *thud*,
spilling over one page. . . .

...and onto the next.

Almost out of energy and ink, Simon and
his friends watched as the beast crept
toward them through the splatter.

It perched silently
above them,
waiting for the right
moment to leap.

SUDDENLY, IT JUMPED AT SIMON!

But to his surprise, the beast gave
him a big, sloppy kiss.

THE MONSTER WAS FRIENDLY!

The foursome collapsed on the
beast's back and headed across the page,
happy and relieved.

When they arrived at the last page, the pens
drew a soft, warm bed and cover, using the
last drop of ink.

Soon after they had been tucked in, Simon
and his new-found friend were asleep.

Then the ink bottle jiggled off
the page like a tired old hermit crab.

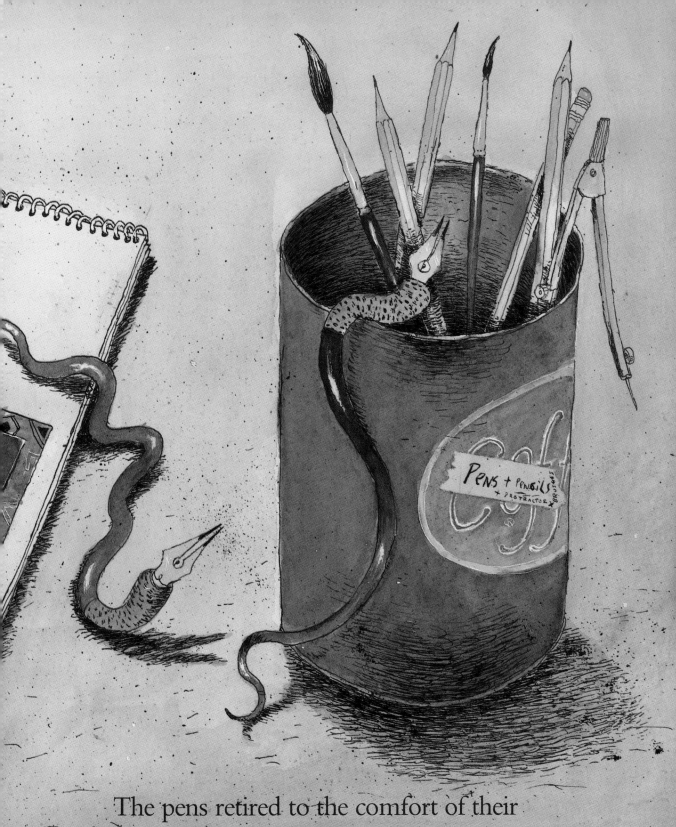

The pens retired to the comfort of their spacious jar, yawned a sigh of relief, and dozed off.

The boy awoke the next morning, fully rested.

To his amazement and delight, there was a book on the table, where he had left the drawing of Simon and the monster the night before.

And that is the same book
that you've just finished reading.